CONTENTS

PARKS AND WRECKS

by Lori Haskins Houran
illustrated by Jessica Warrick

KANE PRESS
New York

Spork

Trixie Lopez

Mrs. Buckle

Jack Donnelly

Grace Hanford

Piper Cho

Adam Novak

Newton Miller

Jo Jo

REPORT TO TROOP

GALAXY SCOUTS

BEEP. BEEP. BEEP.
Guys, guess what! I won a pie-eating contest, and my picture was in the newspaper!
(In case you don't know, a pie is a delicious circular dessert. And a newspaper is how Earthlings share VERY IMPORTANT INFORMATION.)
I don't want to brag, but . . . I'm pretty sure I'm famous now! People are going to follow me around, asking for autographs, taking pictures. . . .
I'd better go polish my antennae. Got to look good for my fans!

1

UP AND DOWN

"What's left, Newton? Anything good?" asked Trixie.

She peeked over Newton's shoulder into the Treasure Box on Mrs. Buckle's desk. It was hard being the last person to pick. Only two things were left in the box. A cool light-up yo-yo . . . and a pack of smiley pencils.

"Ugh! Not the smiley pencils!" Trixie groaned. Everyone knew that was the worst Treasure Box prize. They were just pencils. Who cared if they had smiley faces on them?

"Too bad!" said Jack with a smirk. Trixie wanted to stick out her tongue, but Mrs. Buckle was watching.

"Don't worry, Trixie," Newton said. "You can have the yo-yo."

"Really? Thanks!" said Trixie. "What do you want for it? One of my cookies at lunch?"

"No. That's okay. I don't need anything." Newton handed the yo-yo to Trixie.

"Newton, you're so generous!" said Grace.

"Generous?" Spork took a step back. "That sounds bad. Is it contagious? You should go home, Newton, so you don't get everyone else sick."

"Newton isn't sick," Mrs. Buckle explained. "*Generous* means you give something to someone without wanting anything back."

"So it *is* like being contagious!" said Spork. "If you give someone the Klozidian flu, you definitely don't want it back!"

Trixie couldn't help smiling. Spork had been on Earth for a while now, but he still didn't know lots of things.

"We're not talking about giving away germs," Grace said. "We're talking about nice things. Like the last yo-yo in the Treasure Box. Try it out, Trixie!"

Trixie looped the yo-yo around her finger. She flicked her hand. The yo-yo lit up bright purple as it whizzed up and

down its string. Up, down. Up, down.

Spork still looked confused. "But . . . if you give something nice away, then you don't have it for yourself."

"It can be hard," Mrs. Buckle said. "That's why generosity is so special." She gave Newton a squeeze.

Trixie bit her lip. She felt a little like the yo-yo on her finger. One second she was up. *I got the last yo-yo!* The next second she was down. *Would I have given it away like Newton did? Am I generous, too?*

Luckily, the recess bell cut into her thoughts. Trixie rushed over to the closet and scooped out a kickball.

"Don't forget—we're in the kindergarten yard today!" called Mrs. Buckle as everyone headed outside.

"Oh, right," said Spork. "Our yard's getting new swings!" He followed Trixie to the kindergarten area. They passed a low slide on

the way to a
patch of grass.
"Do you think
there's enough
room for kickball
here?"
"Let's try it." Trixie
rolled the ball to Spork. He
kicked it, and it sailed past her
head—right over a stone wall!

"Oh, glarps! Sometimes I forget how weak Earth's gravity is!" said Spork. He ran to the wall and hopped on top easily.

Trixie couldn't jump that high—Earth's gravity didn't seem weak to her!—but the wall wasn't hard to climb. In a minute she was looking over the top. She spotted the ball, but she had to blink a few times to make sure she wasn't seeing things.

Yup. There was the kickball . . . lying like an egg in a huge stone nest!

2

THE FORGOTTEN PARK

"What is this place?" Spork asked.

They stared at the square of ground below them. Stone walls lined with faded benches bordered it. There was a rusty iron door on one side.

In the middle of the square was a fountain clogged with sticks and leaves. And in the middle of the fountain stood a bird statue. The kickball, resting alongside three stone eggs, looked almost at home in the bird's nest.

"It's a park. Chickadee Park," Trixie
said. "I used to come here with my
mom when I was little. It was so pretty
then. Now it's sort of . . ."

"Sad," Spork finished for her. "It reminds me of Pluto. Nobody visits anymore now that it's just a dwarf planet."

"TRIXIE! SPORK!" called Mrs. Buckle. "What ARE you doing up there?"

"Mrs. Buckle, you'll never believe it!" Trixie told her teacher all about the park. "It used to have rows of pink and yellow flowers. And the fountain would spray really high so you could splash in the water. And it was the best place EVER for picnics. But now it's all lonely and forgotten!"

"A forgotten park?" Mrs. Buckle said.

"Really?" She paused for a second.

Then Mrs. Buckle scrambled up the wall! "Oh, I can tell it was beautiful," she said.

"MRS. BUCKLE!" called Principal Hale. "What ARE you doing up there?"

"Oops," said Mrs. Buckle.

The bell rang, and Trixie followed everyone back into the classroom. She sat down on the rug for Show and Share. But she kept thinking about Chickadee Park. There was nowhere else like it in town. Where did little kids go to splash and have picnics now?

She pictured the iron door. *I wonder . . .*

"All right. Who has something to share?" asked Mrs. Buckle.

"Me! Me!" yelped Spork. He waved his hand so hard his antennae wobbled.

Mrs. Buckle smiled. "Go ahead, Spork."

Spork pulled a clipping out of his pocket. "I was in your Earth newspaper

this morning! This is the most exciting thing to happen since I crash— Er, since I *landed* on your planet! But don't worry. I won't let my fans get in the way of anything."

"Your fans?" said Trixie.

She glanced at the other kids. All of them had been in the newspaper before. Adam had made the sports section just last week with his baseball team. Jack had been on the front page three years in a row for winning the spelling bee.

"Uh, Spork, you're *not* going to have fans following you around," scoffed Jack.

"That's right," Spork said cheerfully. "They won't follow me around. That's because I have a plan. You'll see. Or maybe . . . you WON'T see!" He grinned.

Trixie wasn't sure what Spork meant. But she didn't have time to think about it now, because she was busy making a plan, too.

A plan that involved a rusty iron door into a forgotten park . . . that wasn't forgotten anymore.

3

SECRET MISSION

"Hello?" whispered Trixie.

She pushed the iron door gently. It creaked on its hinges as it swung open. Trixie stepped cautiously into the park.

"Are you sure we're allowed to go in there?" asked Newton.

Jack rolled his eyes. "It's a public park. Of course we can go in." He marched in behind Trixie and tossed his backpack on a bench. Newton and Grace followed.

"Oh, it's cozy!" said Grace. "Look at the fountain! Too bad it doesn't work anymore. It's so pretty."

"This place is special, right?" Trixie said. She plucked the kickball out of the bird's nest. She'd take it back to school tomorrow.

"Yeah. If you ignore the fact that it's totally grubby," Jack said.

"That's the thing," said Trixie, getting excited. "It doesn't *have* to be grubby anymore! This place was . . . lost, in a way. But we can save it!"

"Like a secret rescue mission?" asked Jack. He looked a little more interested now.

"Sure!" Trixie said.

Newton was already kneeling down, poking the ground. "I planted flowers for my science project last year," he said. "I could dig them up and move them here. I think they'd do well in this soil."

"My mom and I have been doing tons of yard work," Grace said. "I'll bring rakes for cleaning up the leaves."

"I've got paint for the benches. I use it to touch up the walls in my spaceship."

"Wait—who said that?" asked Trixie.

ZAP! There was a flash of orange light. Spork appeared, right in front of Grace.

"Spork!" Grace cried. "Where did you come from?"

"I was here all along," said Spork. "I switched to Invisible Mode after school so my fans wouldn't follow me. I told you I had a plan!"

"You can turn *invisible*?" asked Newton.

"Of course!" Spork said. "Earthlings can, too, right? Jack was invisible for two whole days last week."

Jack snorted. "I wasn't invisible. I was *absent*."

"Oh!" said Spork. "Well, it comes in handy. Only, I don't do it much—not since the time on my planet when I was SURE I had put my pants on. But when I switched back . . ."

Spork's orange face turned brighter orange. "Er—so, what else do we need for the park?"

Jack brushed some dirt off a bench. "Heavy-duty scrub brushes, for sure," he said. "We have them at the market where I work on Saturdays. I'll buy

some with my earnings tomorrow and bring them straight to the park."

"Awesome!" Trixie said. "And I'll bring—"

Trixie stopped. What COULD she bring? She and her mom lived in an apartment. They didn't have a yard, so they didn't own outdoor stuff.

She kept wracking her brain. She couldn't think of anything useful she had to give. Not one thing! Everyone was being so generous, even Jack!

Trixie tried to shake off the bad feeling. "Get here when you can tomorrow," she told the others.

I'll be here at sun-up, she thought. *I can't be generous. But I can work harder than anyone!*

4

CLEAN-UP CREW

Trixie barely sat still all weekend.

On Saturday morning, she planted flowers with Newton and painted some park benches with Spork. Spork's Intergalactic Green paint turned out to be . . . interesting. It made the benches shimmer and sparkle in the sunlight. Trixie was pretty sure they'd glow in the dark!

In the afternoon she and Jack

scrubbed the chickadee statue. "Ha, ha!" he kept saying. "We're cleaning bird poop . . . off a *bird*!"

Trixie and Grace wore rain boots on Sunday so they could climb inside the fountain. They started raking clumps of mucky leaves out of the bottom.

"Yikes!" yelped Grace.

Trixie looked over. Grace was dripping wet!

"IT WORKS!" cried Trixie.

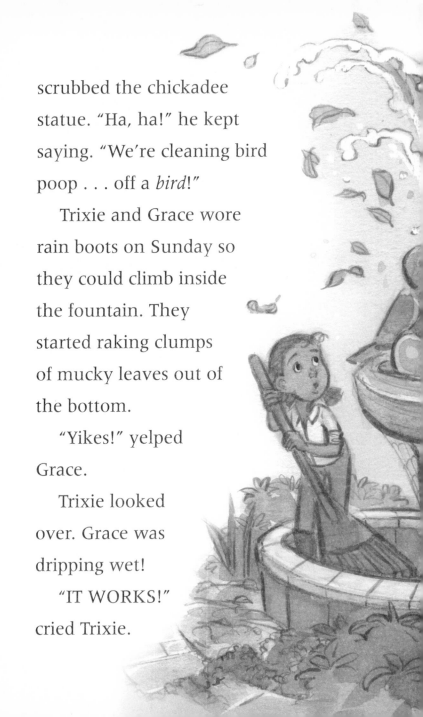

"The fountain WORKS. The
leaves were just blocking
the spouts!"

The girls raked faster.
Soon the fountain was
spraying high, clear
streams of water.

"Just right for
splashing!" Trixie said.
Trixie worked
straight through until
dinner. She was
so tired she could
barely lift her fork!
She woke
up Monday
morning with
sore muscles all

over her body . . . and a smile on her face.

The park had looked so good when she had left the day before. She couldn't wait to see it again.

Trixie sat up in bed. Why not go right now, before school?

She practically skipped to Chickadee Park. But when she got to the iron door, she gasped.

There was a big padlock on the handle!

Trixie tugged it. It was locked tight.

"HEY!" shouted a voice. "What are you doing here?"

Trixie spun around. A park ranger was walking straight toward her.

Oh, no, thought Trixie. *I didn't ask for permission to clean up the park. Maybe I'll get in trouble. Maybe I'll get arrested!*

"You can't go in there, miss," the ranger said. "I got orders to lock up this park. My boss said no one uses it anymore, and it's in rough shape."

The ranger shrugged as he headed back to his truck. "Looks nice to me. Seems a shame to close it up for good."

For good? As in, forever? Trixie felt a lump in her throat.

She took off running. She didn't stop until she reached Mrs. Buckle's classroom.

"Park—orders—closed!" she panted.

"*What?*" said Newton.

"CLOSED?" Jack shouted.

"Hold on! Slow down. What's going on?" asked Mrs. Buckle.

Trixie took a few deep breaths while

Grace told Mrs. Buckle about fixing up
Chickadee Park.

"But now there's a lock on the door,"
Trixie added. "And the park is closed
forever!"

"Oh, my," said Mrs. Buckle. "Let me
see."

They all hurried out to the kindergarten yard. Mrs. Buckle climbed up the stone wall. "Wow! Kids, it looks *incredible*!"

"It was Trixie's idea," said Grace. "We helped. But she did the most."

"Trixie, how generous of you!" Mrs. Buckle said, still admiring the park.

"Generous?" Trixie shook her head sadly. "No, I wasn't generous. Everyone else gave stuff. Newton gave flowers. Spork gave paint. I didn't have anything to give."

"You gave your time and effort," said Mrs. Buckle. "Lots of it. That's generosity, too!"

"It is?" For a moment, Trixie felt great. *I was generous!*

Then she remembered the padlock

on the door. Her generosity hadn't done a bit of good.

"REALLY, Mrs. Buckle? You're climbing that wall *again*?" Principal Hale called.

Mrs. Buckle scooted down. "It's too bad the Parks Director can't get a look at the park now," she said to the kids. "I'm

pretty sure he works in Mayor Tupper's office. . . ."

Trixie remembered Mayor Tupper. She had visited their school a few months ago, and she was really nice. Maybe the Parks Director was nice, too!

"Can't we invite him to see it?" Spork piped in.

"You know, it can't hurt to ask," Mrs. Buckle said. "I'll be right back!"

When Mrs. Buckle came out of the school building, her eyes were shining. "Mr. Knapp agreed to come see the park at four o'clock," she said. "No promises. But if he likes what he sees, who knows!"

Trixie's heart started to thump.

Chickadee Park had a chance!

5

MAKING A SPLASH

"Any minute now," said Trixie, pacing back and forth in front of the park door.

Everyone else looked restless, too. Newton glanced at his watch. Grace bounced on her toes. Mrs. Buckle chewed a fingernail.

"Hey, where's Spork?" Newton asked.

"He's probably invisible," Jack said. "Yo, Spork! Where are you?"

No one answered.

"Huh," said Jack. "I guess he's really not here."

"That must be Mr. Knapp!" Grace cried. She pointed to a man in a crisp uniform striding down the path. Trixie gulped. He didn't look as friendly as Mayor Tupper. Not *nearly*.

"Good afternoon," Mr. Knapp said briskly. He pulled out a ring of keys and opened the iron door.

Trixie watched nervously as Mr. Knapp walked around eyeing the flowers and the fountain. It was hard to tell what he was thinking. He didn't smile. But he didn't frown, either.

He tapped one of the benches. "Not exactly regulation green," he muttered. Then he turned around to face the group. "This is impressive. The park looks the best it has in years. You should be proud."

Trixie felt a wave of joy. *He likes it!*

"So you'll keep the park open?" asked Grace.

"Unfortunately . . . ," Mr. Knapp began.

Trixie's wave of joy crashed.

". . . there just isn't enough money in the town budget for the park. It's one thing to fix it up once. Keeping it maintained gets expensive."

Mr. Knapp's stern face softened for a moment. "If a lot of people used the park, it might be different. The fact is,

no one comes here anymore. I'm very sorry. But I have to say no."

Mr. Knapp's voice echoed in Trixie's ears. *No one comes here anymore. . . . I have to say no. . . .*

Suddenly Trixie heard another voice. A familiar, cheerful one.

"Here we are! Come on in!"

Spork burst through the door—with a whole crowd behind him!

"Oh, isn't this a sweet park!"

"Look at the flowers!"

People kept spilling into Chickadee Park.

"Wow. These benches are BRIGHT!"

"Let's come back for a picnic."

A cluster of little kids ran straight to the fountain and started splashing and laughing.

"Spork, who are all these people?" asked Grace.

"My fans!" said Spork. "I stayed visible after school so they could follow me. I figured, why not show everyone the fixed-up park?"

"He really has fans . . . for eating pie?" grumbled Jack. "I made the front page for acing *potpourri* at the spelling bee. Silent t, double r! No one followed *me* around."

Another Spork fan walked in.

"Mayor Tupper!" said Mr. Knapp.

"Mr. Knapp! Are you a Sporkie, too? I'm hoping our pie champ will autograph this for me." Mayor Tupper pulled a spatula out of her purse.

"Actually, I'm here about the park," Mr. Knapp said.

"The park?" Mayor Tupper looked around. "It's lovely! But isn't this the one we just—"

"Closed," Mr. Knapp said. "Yes. Might I discuss that with you in private?"

Mr. Knapp led Mayor Tupper to the edge of the fountain. Trixie saw he had the same not-smiling, not-frowning look on his face as before. She still had no idea what it meant! Was he asking the mayor to keep the park open—or making sure she kept it closed?

After a few minutes, Mayor Tupper called to the crowd. "Excuse me, folks! May I have your attention?"

Trixie stepped forward on shaky legs. Spork stood beside her. Mrs. Buckle, Grace, Jack, and Newton gathered around, too.

"Glarps!" Spork whispered. "I forgot I'm famous now. I'd better go invisible so everyone pays attention to the mayor!"

Trixie had never seen Spork disappear before. It wasn't all at once, like the way he reappeared. Instead, Spork vanished in pieces, starting at his toes.

Zoop! There went his feet. *Zoop! Zoop! Zoop!* There went his legs, his stomach, his shoulders.

"Whoa!" said Newton.

"Freaky," said Jack.

Mayor Tupper turned around just in time to see Spork's orange head hover in the air. Then—*zoop!*—that vanished, too.

"EEEEEEEK!" Mayor Tupper shrieked. She looked as if she'd seen a ghost!

Trixie watched the mayor take a step back . . . and topple right into the fountain!

Splash!

"Mayor! Are you okay?" Mr. Knapp reached down to pull Mayor Tupper out.

SPLASH! Mr. Knapp fell in, too!

"Oh, no!" cried Spork. He reappeared with his head in his hands. "I ruined everything!"

Trixie covered her face. She was sure Spork was right. Mayor Tupper was going to be so mad. And stern Mr. Knapp? He was going to be *twice* as mad! Even if they *had* been thinking about saying yes to the park, they'd never do it now!

Then Trixie heard someone giggling.

Who on earth was laughing at poor, wet Mayor Tupper and Mr. Knapp?

Trixie looked up. Her mouth dropped. The *mayor* was the one laughing!

Then Mr. Knapp started in, too . . . even louder! The two of them hooted and snorted, slapping their soggy knees!

Finally they calmed down long enough to help each other up.

"I was about to say that we could
tell everyone was enjoying the park,"
Mayor Tupper said. "Especially the kids
splashing in the fountain. We didn't plan
on splashing in it ourselves!"

Her face turned a little more serious.

"Some generous citizens worked hard to save this park. Mr. Knapp and I want to be generous, too. Together, we're going to find room in the budget to keep the park open." She looked right at Trixie. "For good."

Trixie couldn't believe it. Chickadee Park was staying open!

The crowd cheered. Mrs. Buckle wrapped Trixie in a hug. The others took turns giving her high-fives.

"I guess I was right," said Spork. "Generosity *is* contagious!"

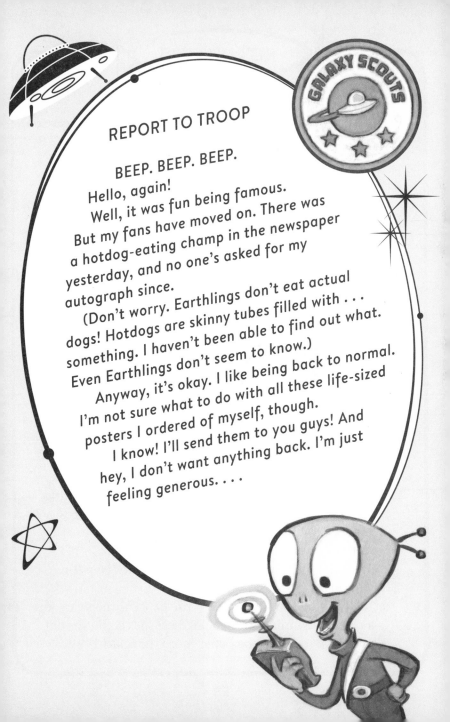

REPORT TO TROOP

BEEP. BEEP. BEEP.

Hello, again!

Well, it was fun being famous. But my fans have moved on. There was a hotdog-eating champ in the newspaper yesterday, and no one's asked for my autograph since.

(Don't worry. Earthlings don't eat actual dogs! Hotdogs are skinny tubes filled with . . . something. I haven't been able to find out what. Even Earthlings don't seem to know.)

Anyway, it's okay. I like being back to normal. I'm not sure what to do with all these life-sized posters I ordered of myself, though.

I know! I'll send them to you guys! And hey, I don't want anything back. I'm just feeling generous. . . .

ACTIVITIES

Greetings!
Captain Astroson is the richest person on my planet, and she's VERY generous! I always hoped I could be as generous as she is, but I thought I had to be rich to do it. Then I learned that you can be generous with your time and energy, too. Did you know that? Take this quiz and see if you know how to be generous.
—Spork

(There can be more than one right answer.)

1. Grace didn't get a prize from the Cosmic Claw Machine and she's feeling sad. What can you do?
   a. Tell Grace not to zoop away. The prize is no big deal.
   b. Give Grace a stretchy blue alien you won playing Digi-Yubble.
   c. Hand Grace a quarter to try a different game.
   d. Suggest Newton give Grace one of his prizes.

2. Newton is excited about being in the paper for winning the science fair. Which of these actions show generosity?
   a. Tell Newton his picture in the article is great.
   b. Cut out the article and tape it to your wall.
   c. Bring in extra copies of the newspaper for Newton to send to his cousins.
   d. Tell Newton that Jack was in the paper three years in a row for winning the spelling bee. Maybe he should set a goal to get in the paper more than Jack!

3. Sharing the Klozidian flu is not the best kind of sharing. How can you be generous to a sick friend?
   a. Stay after school to get your friend's missed work and then head over to his house to give it to him.
   b. Invite your friend to the playground to play.
   c. Reschedule the sleepover you had planned for after he's feeling better.
   d. Bring him tissues and some pluppleberry juice.

4. Mrs. Buckle's class wants to keep Chickadee Park looking wonderful. Each student wants to help. Which students are generous?
   a. Newton collects trash at the park each week during the summer.
   b. Trixie uses her birthday money to buy a hummingbird feeder for the park.
   c. Grace asks her aunt, who is a florist, to donate flowers so that she can plant them at the park.
   d. Jack puts up flyers around town encouraging more people to volunteer.

Answers:
1. You can be generous by choosing *b* or *c*. Telling Newton to share one of his prizes would show his generosity, not yours, so don't choose *d*. Trying to get Grace to not feel bad is kind, but it doesn't show generosity, so *a* isn't the best choice, either.
2. Finding more copies of the newspaper for Newton is generous, so *c* is the best answer.
3. Generosity and kindness are all on display in *a*, *c*, and *d*. Most people (and aliens!) with the flu need to rest, so *b* isn't great.
4. You can be generous with time, effort, or money, so *a*, *b*, *c*, and *d* are all good answers.

Scrambled Snacks

After the mayor said the park could stay open, Mrs. Buckle's class had a potluck picnic in the park to celebrate.

Unscramble the underlined words to find out what each student brought.

Trixie brought shiny red **pleaps** she had just picked at the orchard.

Newton brought **rckcares nda hecese**—two different kinds! Cheddar and swiss.

Grace brought **psihc**. She likes them more than pretzels.

Jack brought **mnlwaoeert**. He made sure to tell Spork not to spit the seeds.

Spork brought **dsenacshwi**. He wanted his friends to try his favorite, moon butter and jelly.

Answer: Trixie brought apples. Newton brought crackers and cheese. Grace brought chips. Jack brought watermelon. Spork brought sandwiches. (The moon butter turned out to be a little chalky for Earthling taste buds. But the pluppleberry jelly was a hit!)

MEET THE AUTHOR AND ILLUSTRATOR

LORI HASKINS HOURAN has written more than twenty books for kids (not counting the ones her flarg ate). She lives in Massachusetts with five silly aliens who claim to be her family.

JESSICA WARRICK has illustrated lots of picture books about dogs, cats, and kids, but she is mostly interested in drawing aliens, for some strange reason. She does a pretty good job acting like an Earthling . . . most of the time.

Spork just landed on Earth, and look, he already has lots of fans!

★ **Moonbeam Children's Book Awards Gold Medal**
Best Book Series—Chapter Books

★ **Moonbeam Children's Book Awards Silver Medal**
Juvenile Fiction—Early Reader/Chapter Books
for book #1 *Spork Out of Orbit*

"Young readers are going to love this series! Spork is a funny and unexpected main character. Kids will love his antics and sweet disposition. Teachers and parents will appreciate the subtle messages embedded in the stories. The kids in the stories genuinely like each other, which I found refreshing. I will be giving these books to my young friends."—**Ron Roy**, author of A to Z Mysteries, Calendar Mysteries, and Capital Mysteries

"A breezy, humorous lesson in honesty that never stoops to didacticism. The other three volumes publishing simultaneously address similarly weighty lessons—lying, shyness, bullying, and responsibility—all with a multicultural cast of Everykids. . . . A good choice for those new to chapters."
—**Kirkus** for book #1 *Spork Out of Orbit*

"This is a book where readers, kids, and aliens learn together, experiencing how words and choices affect all of us. It's simple, elegant, and very insightful storytelling. *Greetings, Sharkling!* doesn't waste a single page of opportunity."
—**The San Francisco Book Review**

"I'm so glad Spork landed on Earth! His misadventures are playful and sweet, and I love the clever wordplay!"
—**Becca Zerkin**, former children's book reviewer for the *New York Times Book Review* and *School Library Journal*

"Kids will love reading about Spork. Parents, teachers, and librarians will love reading aloud this series to those same kids."—**Rob Reid**, author of *Silly Books to Read Aloud*

How to Be an Earthling
Winner of the Moonbeam Gold Medal
for Best Chapter Book Series!

Respect   **Honesty**   **Responsibility**   **Courage**

Kindness   **Perseverance**   **Citizenship**   **Self-Control**

Patience   **Generosity**   **Acceptance**   **Cooperation**

To learn more about Spork, go to kanepress.com

Check out these other series from Kane Press

Animal Antics A to Z® (Grades PreK–2 • Ages 3–8)
Winner of two *Learning* Magazine Teachers' Choice Awards
"A great product for any class learning about letters!"
—*Teachers' Choice Award reviewer comment*

Holidays & Heroes (Grades 1–4 • Ages 6–10)
"Commemorates the influential figures behind important American celebrations. This volume emphasizes the importance of lofty ambitions and fortitude in the face of adversity…"—*Booklist* (for *Let's Celebrate Martin Luther King Jr. Day*)

Let's Read Together® (Grades PreK–3 • Ages 4–8)
"Storylines are silly and inventive, and recall Dr. Seuss's *Cat in the Hat* for the building of rhythm and rhyming words."—*School Library Journal*

Makers Make It Work™ (Grades K–3 • Ages 5–8)
Fun easy-to-read stories tied into the growing Makers Movement.

Math Matters® (Grades K–3 • Ages 5–8)
Winner of a *Learning* Magazine Teachers' Choice Award
"These cheerfully illustrated titles offer primary-grade children practice in math as well as reading."—*Booklist*

The Milo & Jazz Mysteries® (Grades 2–5 • Ages 7–11)
"Gets it just right."—*Booklist,* starred review (for *The Case of the Stinky Socks*); *Book Links'* Best New Books for the Classroom

Mouse Math® (Grades PreK & up • Ages 4 & up)
"The Mouse Math series is a great way to integrate math and literacy into your early childhood curriculum. My students thoroughly enjoyed these books."—*Teaching Children Mathematics*

Science Solves It!® (Grades K–3 • Ages 5–8)
"The Science Solves It! series is a wonderful tool for the elementary teacher who wants to integrate reading and science."—*National Science Teachers Association*

Social Studies Connects® (Grades K–3 • Ages 5–8)
"This series is very strongly recommended…."—*Children's Bookwatch*
"Well done!"—*School Library Journal*

KANEPRESS.com